NAVIGATING ADOLESCENCE

A GUIDE TO TEEN MENTAL HEALTH & WELL-BEING

PIYUSH RAJ

ISBN 979-8-89026-844-0

TABLE OF CONTENTS

INTRODUCTION

* In today's fast-paced and interconnected world, teenagers are confronted with an array of challenges that impact their mental health and well-being. This book, "Navigating Adolescence," aims to shed light on the pressing mental health issues faced by teenagers and offers practical guidance and support for both teenagers and the adults who care for them. By addressing topics such as anxiety, depression, stress, cyberbullying, body image, substance abuse, and relationship issues, this book aims to foster understanding, awareness, and resilience in the face of these challenges.

ACKNOWLEDGEMENT

We would like to express our deepest gratitude to all those who have contributed to the creation of this book on the critical topic of mental health issues faced by teenagers in today's generation. The exploration of the challenges they encounter, often underappreciated or overlooked by society, has been a collective effort driven by a shared commitment to improving the well-being of young individuals.

First and foremost, we extend our appreciation to the teenagers who bravely shared their experiences and stories, providing invaluable insights into the complex landscape of mental health. Your courage and resilience inspire us, and it is our hope that this book will amplify your voices and contribute to a greater understanding and empathy among readers.

We would also like to acknowledge the extensive research conducted in the field of mental health, as well as the experts, psychologists, and counselors who have dedicated their knowledge and expertise to shed light on these pressing issues. Your contributions have provided the foundation upon which this book stands, ensuring its accuracy and relevance.

Furthermore, we extend our thanks to the parents, teachers, and mentors who play a vital role in the lives of teenagers. Your guidance, support, and advocacy are crucial in creating a nurturing environment that fosters positive mental health and well-being. Your dedication to the emotional and psychological welfare of the next generation is invaluable.

Lastly, we express our gratitude to society as a whole. It is through open dialogue, the breaking down of stigmas, and the creation of safe spaces that we can collectively address these challenges. By acknowledging the importance of mental health, actively working towards prevention, and providing accessible resources, we can offer teenagers the support they need to thrive in the face of adversity.

This book aims to raise awareness, spark conversations, and promote a compassionate approach to addressing mental health issues faced by teenagers. It is our sincere hope that it will serve as a catalyst for change, inspiring individuals and communities to prioritize the well-being of our youth and create a brighter, more supportive future.

Thank you for joining us on this journey of understanding and empowerment.

Sincerely,

Piyush Raj

ABOUT AUTHOR

Hello, my name is Piyush Raj and I am a proud son of my amazing parents and a loving brother to two wonderful sisters. I am an avid traveler and a passionate biker who enjoys exploring new places on two wheels.

As the founder of Beckon Social Media Agency, I am dedicated to helping entrepreneurs like myself succeed in the ever-changing world of social media. With a wealth of experience in this field, I am committed to providing the best possible solutions to my clients, helping them to achieve their business goals and thrive in today's digital landscape.

Driven by a deep desire to make a difference in the lives of others, I am constantly seeking new ways to innovate and improve the services that I offer. Whether you are a small business owner or a large corporation, I am here to help you achieve your marketing objectives and take your brand to new heights.

So if you're looking for a reliable and experienced social media expert to help you navigate the complexities of the digital world, look no further than Beckon Social Media Agency. I am here to help you succeed, every step of the way. for more info you can read this.

THE AUTHORS LIFE JOURNEY

*** New Beginning**

- [ ] It was a crisp autumn morning when I stepped into the world of adolescence. My teenage years awaited, filled with hopes, dreams, and a burning desire to make my mark on the world. The halls of my high school were buzzing with energy, and I was determined to find my place among the sea of faces.

*** Friends and Foes**

- [ ] Navigating the treacherous waters of high school friendships was no easy feat. I encountered a diverse group of individuals, each with their own quirks and complexities. Some friendships bloomed effortlessly, while others fizzled out, leaving me with valuable lessons about trust and loyalty. Together, we weathered the storms of teenage drama, forging unbreakable bonds along the way.

*** Discovering Passions**

- [ ] Amidst the chaos of teenage life, I stumbled upon my true passions. Through trial and error, I explored various activities, from sports to arts, searching for that one thing that would set my soul ablaze. It was on the stage, under the spotlight, that I found my voice and discovered the transformative power of art. Whether it was acting, singing, or dancing, the stage became my refuge, and my passion ignited a fire within me.

* Overcoming Obstacles

- [ ] Life has its way of throwing unexpected challenges our way, and my teenage years were no exception. I faced setbacks, failures, and moments of self-doubt that tested my resilience. Yet, through perseverance and the support of my loved ones, I learned to rise above adversity. Each setback became an opportunity for growth, molding me into a stronger and more resilient individual.

* Love and Heartbreak

- [ ] Ah, young love—a rollercoaster of emotions that can both exhilarate and devastate. In the realm of teenage romance, I experienced the euphoria of falling in love and the heartache of heartbreak. Through the ups and downs of relationships, I learned about the importance of communication, compromise, and self-love. These experiences shaped my understanding of love and set the stage for healthier relationships in the future.

* Self-Discovery

- [ ] As I journeyed through my teenage years, I embarked on a quest of self-discovery. I asked myself tough questions and delved deep into my identity, exploring my beliefs, passions, and dreams. Through introspection and self-reflection, I gained a clearer sense of who I truly was and what I aspired to become. I embraced my quirks, accepted my flaws, and learned to love myself unconditionally.

*The Road Ahead

- [ ] As my teenage years drew to a close, I stood on the precipice of adulthood, ready to embark on new adventures. The future shimmered with infinite possibilities, and I knew that the lessons I learned during my teenage journey would guide me forward. With hope in my heart and a hunger for life, I set my sights on the horizon, eager to embrace the challenges and triumphs that awaited me.

*Epilogue: Reflections

- [ ] Now, as I look back on my teenage years, I am filled with gratitude for the experiences that shaped me into the person I am today. The journey was not always smooth, but it was undoubtedly transformative. I carry the memories, the friendships, and the lessons with me as I step into adulthood, forever grateful for the teenage tale that unfolded and the person it allowed me to become.

Chapter 1

—◆◆◆—

UNDERSTANDING TEENAGE MENTAL HEALTH

Introduction:

In this chapter, we delve into the prevalence and impact of mental health issues among teenagers. We explore the factors contributing to these challenges, the importance of early intervention and seeking help, and address the stigma surrounding mental health. By understanding the depth of the problem, we can work towards effective solutions and support systems for teenagers. In a world that seems to be constantly changing, one thing remains constant—the challenges faced by teenagers as they navigate through their formative years. The teenage phase is often seen as a time of growth, self-discovery, and excitement. However, it is also a period marked by unique mental health challenges. In this chapter, we will delve into the prevalence and impact of mental health issues among teenagers, explore the factors that contribute to these challenges, highlight the importance of early intervention, and address the stigma surrounding mental health.

Motivation and Inspiration

As I sit down to write this book, I am motivated by a deep concern for the well-being of teenagers around the world. The teenage years are a time of immense change and growth, but they can also be filled with challenges and difficulties. One aspect of adolescent life that I find particularly important to address is mental health. The prevalence and impact of mental health issues among teenagers have been on the rise, and it is crucial that we understand the underlying factors contributing to these challenges. Through this book, I hope to shed light on the topic, inspire open conversations, and provide guidance for teenagers, parents, educators, and anyone interested in supporting the mental well-being of young people.

Real-Life Story: Emma's Struggle

Emma, a bright and talented sixteen-year-old, seemed to have it all together. She excelled academically, had a strong circle of friends, and was actively involved in extracurricular activities. From the outside, it appeared that Emma had the perfect teenage life. However, beneath the surface, Emma was silently struggling with her mental health.

Pressure to succeed academically, coupled with the demands of a competitive sports team, left Emma feeling overwhelmed. She started experiencing constant anxiety, difficulty sleeping, and a loss of interest in activities she once enjoyed. Fearful of being judged or labeled as weak,

Emma kept her struggles hidden, putting on a brave face and pretending that everything was okay.

Months passed, and Emma's mental health deteriorated further. She began withdrawing from her friends and isolating herself from social activities. Her academic performance suffered, and she found it increasingly challenging to concentrate and complete her schoolwork. Emma's parents noticed the changes in their daughter but were unsure how to address the situation, as they were unaware of the depth of her internal struggle.

One day, overwhelmed by her emotions, Emma finally reached her breaking point. She found solace in a trusted teacher, who recognized her distress and encouraged her to seek professional help. Through therapy and support, Emma began to navigate her way towards recovery. It was a difficult journey, but with time and the right interventions, Emma gradually regained her mental well-being and rediscovered her passion for life.

Emma's story is just one example of the countless teenagers who silently battle mental health challenges. It highlights the urgency and importance of understanding teenage mental health, as well as the need for early intervention and support. By breaking the stigma surrounding mental health and fostering open conversations, we can create an environment where teenagers like Emma feel safe to seek help and find the support they need.

Section 1: The Rising Tide of Teenage Mental Health Issues

The Prevalence and Impact of Mental Health Issues Among Teenagers

Teenage mental health issues are more common than we might realize. The pressures of academic expectations, social relationships, and personal identity can all take a toll on a teenager's well-being. According to recent studies, one in five teenagers experiences a mental health disorder. Depression, anxiety, self-harm, eating disorders, and substance abuse are some of the prevalent issues that adolescents face.

Real-life Thoughts: Sarah's Story

Sarah was a vibrant and outgoing teenager, but she often felt overwhelmed and anxious. She struggled with self-doubt, constantly comparing herself to her peers on social media. Eventually, Sarah sought help and discovered that she was not alone. Her story serves as a reminder that mental health challenges can affect anyone, regardless of outward appearances.

1.1 The Scope of the Problem

Statistics and research highlighting the prevalence of mental health issues among teenagers

Common mental health disorders: anxiety, depression, eating disorders, self-harm, etc.

Exploring the impact of untreated mental health issues on academic performance, relationships, and overall well-being

1.2 Factors Contributing to Teenage Mental Health Challenges

Academic pressure and high expectations

Social media and digital culture

Bullying and peer pressure

Family dynamics and relationships

Traumatic experiences and adverse childhood events

Biological and genetic factors

Section 2: The Importance of Early Intervention and Seeking Help

Factors Contributing to Teenage Mental Health Challenges

Several factors contribute to teenage mental health challenges. Academic pressure, societal expectations, family dynamics, hormonal changes, and genetic predispositions all play a role. It is crucial to recognize that these challenges are multifaceted and can vary from person to person.

Real-life Thoughts: Alex's Experience

Alex had always been an excellent student, but the mounting pressure to perform well in exams began to take a toll on his mental health. He felt overwhelmed and constantly anxious. However, with the support of his family and a shift in perspective, Alex was able to find a balance between academic success and his overall well-being.

2.1 Recognizing the Signs and Symptoms

Understanding the manifestations of common mental health issues in teenagers

Behavioral, emotional, and physical indicators

The importance of open communication and active listening

2.2 Breaking the Silence: Encouraging Help-Seeking Behaviors

Educating teenagers, parents, educators, and communities about mental health

Promoting mental health literacy and destigmatizing seeking help

Providing information on available resources and support systems

Encouraging peer support and mentorship programs

Section 3: Addressing the Stigma Surrounding Mental Health

The Importance of Early Intervention and Seeking Help

Early intervention is key when it comes to addressing teenage mental health issues. It is essential for parents, educators, and society as a whole to be proactive in identifying and supporting teenagers who may be struggling. Seeking help from mental health professionals can provide the necessary guidance and support for teenagers to navigate their challenges effectively.

Real-life Thoughts: Emily's Journey

Emily battled with depression throughout her teenage years. She initially hesitated to seek help, fearing judgment and stigma. However, when she finally reached out to a counselor, she found a safe space to express her feelings and receive the support she needed. Emily's journey illustrates the importance of early intervention and the positive impact it can have on a teenager's life.

3.1 Challenging Stereotypes and Misconceptions

Understanding the origins of mental health stigma

Dispelling myths about mental illness

Sharing personal stories of resilience and recovery

3.2 Promoting Mental Health Awareness and Advocacy

The role of media, schools, and communities in raising awareness

Educating the public about mental health and its impact on teenagers

Advocating for policy changes and increased funding for mental health services

Section 4: Solution-Oriented Approaches

Addressing the Stigma Surrounding Mental Health

Stigma surrounding mental health remains a significant barrier for teenagers seeking help. By educating ourselves and promoting open conversations about mental health, we can work towards creating a more accepting and supportive environment. Destigmatizing mental health issues will enable teenagers to seek help without fear of judgment or isolation.

Real-life Thoughts: Jake's Struggle

Jake battled with anxiety for years but felt unable to discuss his challenges due to the stigma surrounding mental health. Eventually, Jake found solace in a support group that provided him with a sense of belonging and understanding. Jake's story reminds us of the importance of creating safe spaces for teenagers to share their experiences and find support.

4.1 Integrating Mental Health Education into Schools

Implementing comprehensive mental health curriculum

Training educators and staff on recognizing signs of distress

Providing access to school counselors and mental health professionals

4.2 Enhancing Community Support Systems

Developing partnerships between schools, healthcare providers, and community organizations

Establishing youth-friendly mental health services and helplines

Creating safe spaces for open dialogue and support groups

4.3 Encouraging Holistic Approaches to Treatment and Support

The importance of therapy, medication, and other evidence-based treatments

Promoting self-care, mindfulness, and stress reduction techniques

Engaging in physical activity and healthy lifestyle choices

Fostering a supportive network of friends, family, and mentors

Conclusion:

Understanding teenage mental health is a crucial step in promoting well-being and resilience among young individuals. By acknowledging the prevalence and impact of mental health issues, recognizing the contributing factors, emphasizing early intervention, and addressing the stigma, we can create a society that Understanding the prevalence and impact of mental health issues among teenagers is the first step towards creating effective solutions and support systems. By addressing the factors contributing to these challenges, emphasizing the importance of early intervention and seeking help, and actively working to reduce stigma, we can pave the way for a healthier future for our teenagers. Through collaboration and a commitment to mental health, we can create an environment that fosters resilience, empathy, and understanding.

Chapter 2

ANXIETY, DEPRESSION, AND STRESS

Introduction:

This chapter explores the challenges of anxiety, depression, and stress among teenagers. It aims to provide a comprehensive understanding of these conditions and their impact on well-being. By delving into their causes, symptoms, and effects, this chapter equips readers with practical strategies to manage and reduce their impact.

Key points:

Defining anxiety, depression, and stress and highlighting their distinct features.

Exploring the diverse ways these conditions can manifest in teenagers' lives.

Coping strategies, including self-care practices and cognitive behavioral techniques.

Building resilience through strengths, healthy coping mechanisms, and a growth mindset.

The role of therapy, medication, and support networks in seeking help and guidance.

Motivation and Inspiration:

In a world filled with constant demands and pressures, it is no wonder that anxiety, depression, and stress have become increasingly prevalent. The burden of these mental health challenges can weigh heavily on individuals, affecting their overall well-being and quality of life. However, it is essential to recognize that there is hope and that there are effective strategies for managing and overcoming these difficulties. This chapter aims to provide a comprehensive understanding of anxiety, depression, and stress, as well as offer practical guidance on coping mechanisms, building resilience, and seeking support.

Real-Life Story: Sarah's Struggle

Sarah was always known as a cheerful and outgoing person. Her infectious laughter could brighten up anyone's day, and her presence filled a room with warmth. However, behind her vibrant smile, Sarah was silently battling with anxiety and depression. Her journey with mental health challenges began during her teenage years when she started feeling overwhelmed by the mounting expectations and pressures of school, friendships, and family.

Sarah's anxiety manifested as a constant worry that gnawed at her thoughts. She would lie awake at night, her mind racing with irrational fears and scenarios of impending doom. Her heart would race, her palms would sweat, and she would struggle to catch her breath. Each day felt like a daunting mountain to climb, and it took a tremendous effort for her to put on a brave face and face the world.

Depression gradually engulfed Sarah, casting a dark cloud over her life. She began experiencing a profound sadness that seemed to penetrate every aspect of her being. Simple tasks became monumental challenges, and she lost interest in activities she once loved. Sarah often found herself in a state of emotional numbness, unable to derive pleasure from the things that used to bring her joy. The weight of her depression grew heavier with each passing day.

Recognizing Symptoms and Seeking Help:

One of the critical steps in overcoming anxiety, depression, and stress is recognizing the symptoms and acknowledging the need for help. Sarah's journey toward recovery began when she confided in a trusted friend about her struggles. Her friend listened with compassion and encouraged her to seek professional help. It was then that Sarah realized she wasn't alone in her battle and that there were resources available to support her.

Section 1: Understanding Anxiety, Depression, and Stress

1.1 Defining Anxiety, Depression, and Stress

Exploring the characteristics and symptoms of anxiety, depression, and stress

Differentiating between normal levels and clinical conditions

Understanding the impact of these conditions on overall well-being

1.2 Recognizing Symptoms and Signs

Identifying common physical, emotional, and behavioral symptoms of anxiety, depression, and stress

Discussing the importance of self-awareness and seeking professional help for accurate diagnosis

Breaking the stigma surrounding mental health and encouraging open conversations

Defining and Recognizing Symptoms:

Emily's story echoes the experiences of many who suffer from anxiety, depression, and stress. It is essential to understand the signs and symptoms of these conditions to recognize when we or our loved ones may be in need of support. Anxiety often manifests as persistent worrying, restlessness, irritability, and a constant sense of unease. Depression can bring feelings of sadness, hopelessness, loss of interest in activities, changes in appetite and sleep patterns, and even thoughts of self-harm. Stress can manifest physically, with symptoms such as headaches, muscle tension, fatigue, and sleep disturbances. Recognizing these symptoms is the first step towards seeking help and embarking on a path to recovery.

Section 2: Coping Strategies for Managing and Reducing Anxiety, Depression, and Stress

2.1 Self-Care Practices for Mental Well-being

Establishing a self-care routine that includes activities promoting relaxation, self-reflection, and emotional regulation

Encouraging healthy lifestyle choices, such as regular exercise, balanced nutrition, and sufficient sleep

Exploring the benefits of mindfulness, meditation, and deep breathing exercises in managing symptoms

2.2 Cognitive Behavioral Techniques

Understanding the connection between thoughts, emotions, and behaviors

Introducing cognitive restructuring to challenge negative thought patterns and promote positive thinking

Utilizing problem-solving skills and stress management techniques to address triggers and find effective solutions

2.3 Emotion Regulation and Expressive Therapies

Exploring the role of emotions in anxiety, depression, and stress

Learning techniques for identifying and expressing emotions in healthy ways, such as journaling, art therapy, or music therapy

Developing skills to regulate and manage overwhelming emotions through relaxation exercises and grounding techniques

Coping Strategies:

Emily knew that she needed to develop coping strategies to manage her anxiety, depression, and stress. Through research and consultation with mental health professionals, she discovered a range of techniques that could help her regain control of her life. These included relaxation exercises, such as deep breathing and meditation, which helped calm her racing thoughts. She also found solace in engaging in physical activities like yoga and jogging, which provided a much-needed release of tension. Journaling became a valuable tool for self-reflection, enabling her to express her emotions freely. Emily also learned the importance of setting boundaries and prioritizing self-care, ensuring she had time for activities she enjoyed and surrounded herself with supportive people.

Section 3: Building Resilience and Developing Healthy Coping Mechanisms

3.1 Enhancing Resilience

Understanding the concept of resilience and its role in overcoming adversity

Identifying personal strengths and resources for resilience-building

Promoting a growth mindset and reframing challenges as opportunities for growth and learning

3.2 Social Support Networks

Highlighting the importance of social connections in managing anxiety, depression, and stress

Nurturing healthy relationships and seeking support from trusted individuals

Discussing the benefits of joining support groups or seeking peer support for shared experiences and validation

3.3 Developing Healthy Coping Mechanisms

Encouraging the exploration of healthy coping strategies, such as engaging in hobbies, practicing relaxation techniques, or seeking nature

Educating on the risks and ineffectiveness of maladaptive coping mechanisms, such as substance abuse or self-harm

Building adaptive coping skills, including problem-solving, assertiveness, and emotion regulation, to navigate challenging situations

Building Resilience and Healthy Coping Mechanisms:

As Emily began to implement these coping strategies, she gradually built resilience. Resilience is the ability to bounce back from adversity and grow stronger through life's challenges. Through therapy, Emily discovered that reframing her negative thoughts and developing a more positive mindset was instrumental in her journey to recovery. She also learned to challenge her perfectionism and embrace self-compassion. By accepting that setbacks were a natural part of life, Emily was able to adapt and find healthier ways to cope with stressors.

Section 4: The Role of Therapy, Medication, and Support Networks

4.1 Therapy Options and Approaches

Exploring different types of therapy, such as cognitive-behavioral therapy (CBT), dialectical behavior therapy (DBT), or mindfulness-based therapies

Discussing the benefits of therapy in providing a safe and supportive space for exploring thoughts, emotions, and coping strategies

Addressing common concerns or misconceptions about therapy and promoting its accessibility

4.2 Medication and Psychiatric Support

Explaining the role of medication in treating anxiety, depression, and stress disorders

Highlighting the importance of professional evaluation, diagnosis, and ongoing monitoring when considering medication

Encouraging open communication with healthcare providers and addressing concerns regarding medication

4.3 Support Networks and Resources

Identifying local or online support networks, helplines, and crisis hotlines for immediate assistance

Discussing the value of community resources, such as counseling centers, mental health organizations, or school counseling services

Providing information on self-help books,

The Role of Therapy, Medication, and Support Networks:

While coping strategies were valuable, Emily recognized the importance of seeking professional help. Therapy provided her with a safe space to explore her emotions, gain insights into the underlying causes of her anxiety and depression, and learn effective strategies to manage her symptoms. In some cases, medication may be prescribed by a qualified healthcare provider to alleviate symptoms. Furthermore, support networks, such as friends, family, or support groups, played a crucial role in Emily's recovery. Their understanding, empathy, and encouragement provided her with a sense of belonging and strengthened her resolve to overcome her challenges.

Conclusion:

This chapter empowers teenagers to navigate anxiety, depression, and stress by providing knowledge, tools, and support. By fostering understanding, resilience, and proactive approaches to mental well-being, readers are encouraged to face these challenges, emerge stronger, and thrive in their lives. Emily's journey of resilience serves as a testament to the power of recognizing and addressing anxiety, depression, and stress. By defining the symptoms, exploring coping strategies, building resilience, and seeking therapy, medication, and support networks, individuals can embark on a transformative path towards improved mental well-being. Remember, you are not alone in your struggles, and there is always hope for a brighter future.

Chapter 3

CYBERBULLYING AND ONLINE HARASSMENT

Introduction:

In this chapter, we will delve deep into the issue of cyberbullying and online harassment, shedding light on its nature, consequences, and impact on mental health. We will explore strategies for preventing and addressing cyberbullying, as well as promoting digital well-being and responsible online behavior. By understanding the underlying thoughts behind cyberbullying and offering effective solutions, we can work towards creating a safer online environment for teenagers.

Motivation:

In today's interconnected world, the internet has become an integral part of our lives. It has revolutionized the way we communicate, share information, and connect with others. However, with the immense benefits of technology, there are also dark corners that have emerged, where cyberbullying and online harassment thrive. This chapter aims to shed light on the nature and consequences of these harmful behaviors, recognize their impact on mental health, and provide strategies for prevention and intervention. By understanding these issues and promoting digital well-being, we can create a safer and more compassionate online environment.

Inspiration:

We live in a time where people are more connected than ever before, yet loneliness, depression, and anxiety are on the rise. The advent of social media and online platforms has provided us with opportunities to engage with a vast network of individuals, but it has also exposed us to new forms of cruelty and harassment. It is disheartening to witness the detrimental effects that cyberbullying and online harassment have on individuals, especially young people who are vulnerable to these behaviors. By raising awareness and providing guidance, we can empower victims and bystanders to take a stand against these acts of aggression and promote a culture of respect and kindness online.

Real-Life Story:

Sarah's Story: A Journey from Victim to Advocate

Sarah was a talented high school student who excelled in academics and extracurricular activities. With a passion for art and a drive to make a difference in the world, she used social media as a platform to share her creations and ideas. Sarah believed that the online world could be a source of inspiration and support, but little did she know that it could also become a breeding ground for cruelty.

It started innocently enough – a few mean comments on her posts. Initially, she brushed them off, thinking they were just the result of jealousy or random trolls. However, as time went on, the comments escalated into a relentless stream of insults, threats, and personal attacks. Sarah's confidence shattered, and she felt increasingly isolated and anxious.

Unable to escape the online torment, Sarah's mental health deteriorated. She began to doubt her abilities, questioning her worth as an artist and as a person. Her once vibrant passion turned into a source of fear and self-doubt. The toxic environment that had consumed her online world was seeping into her real life, affecting her relationships and academic performance.

But one day, Sarah decided enough was enough. She mustered the courage to confide in a trusted teacher, who recognized the signs of cyberbullying and online harassment. Together, they reached out to the school administration, who took immediate action to address the situation. Sarah also found solace in support groups and counseling, where she connected with other survivors and learned strategies to heal and rebuild her self-esteem.

Inspired by her own journey of resilience, Sarah became an advocate for digital well-being and responsible online behavior. She joined forces with organizations dedicated to combating cyberbullying, sharing her story to raise awareness and provide resources to others experiencing similar struggles. Sarah discovered that she had the power to turn her pain into purpose, making a positive impact in the lives of countless individuals who needed guidance and support.

Understanding the Nature and Consequences of Cyberbullying:

Cyberbullying refers to the act of using digital communication platforms to intimidate, harass, or target others. It can take various forms, such as spreading rumors, sharing private information, posting hurtful comments, or creating fake profiles with the intention to harm. The anonymity and wide reach of the internet often embolden cyberbullies, making it difficult for victims to escape the torment.

The consequences of cyberbullying can be severe, impacting the mental health and well-being of victims. Victims may experience increased levels of stress, anxiety, depression, and even contemplate self-harm or suicide. It can also lead to social isolation, damaged self-esteem, academic difficulties, and strained relationships with family and friends. Recognizing the signs of online harassment is crucial for early intervention and support.

Motivation and Inspiration:

The rise of the digital age has brought about numerous advancements in technology and communication. However, along with the benefits, there are also darker sides to this virtual world. Cyberbullying and online harassment have become prevalent issues, affecting individuals of all ages and backgrounds. The motivation behind exploring this topic is to shed light on the nature and consequences of such harmful behaviors, raise awareness, and offer guidance on prevention and intervention.

Real-Life Story: Amy's Struggle

Amy was a bright and cheerful teenager who loved spending time online, connecting with friends and exploring new interests. However, her life took a dramatic turn when she became the target of cyberbullying. It started with hurtful comments on her social media posts, accusing her of being unworthy of attention and popularity. Gradually, the harassment escalated, with anonymous messages and even doctored images of Amy circulating online.

The relentless online attacks took a toll on Amy's mental health. She became withdrawn, anxious, and constantly on edge. The once vibrant girl began to doubt her self-worth and struggled with depression. It was a difficult time for Amy, and her parents were at a loss as to how to help her. Recognizing the severity of the situation, they reached out to the school counselor, who provided guidance and support.

Amy's story serves as a powerful reminder of the devastating effects of cyberbullying. It highlights the urgent need for understanding and addressing this issue.

Recognizing Signs of Online Harassment and Its Impact on Mental Health:

Some signs that a teenager may be experiencing online harassment include changes in behavior, sudden withdrawal from social activities, reluctance to use digital devices or engage online, unexplained emotional distress, declining academic performance, or displaying signs of depression or anxiety. It is essential for parents, educators, and friends to remain vigilant and observant, as victims of cyberbullying often suffer in silence.

The impact on mental health can be devastating. Victims of cyberbullying may experience feelings of fear, helplessness, shame, and humiliation. The persistent and invasive nature of online harassment can erode their self-esteem, leading to self-doubt and negative self-perception. It is crucial to provide support and resources to help victims cope with the emotional toll cyberbullying takes on their mental health.

Motivation and Inspiration:

To effectively combat cyberbullying and online harassment, it is crucial to recognize the signs of these harmful behaviors and understand their impact on mental health. This section aims to empower individuals with knowledge to identify when someone is being targeted and provide insights into the psychological consequences of such harassment.

Real-Life Story: Mark's Silent Suffering

Mark, a successful professional in his mid-thirties, was known for his charismatic personality and strong work ethic. However, beneath his confident exterior, Mark was silently battling the torment of online harassment. A disgruntled colleague had taken their rivalry to the digital realm, creating anonymous social media accounts solely dedicated to defaming Mark.

With time, Mark's self-esteem plummeted, and he became increasingly isolated. The relentless barrage of false accusations and malicious rumors affected not only his professional reputation but also his personal relationships. The constant fear of being judged and the inability to escape the harassment online took a toll on Mark's mental well-being.

Mark's story demonstrates how online harassment can impact individuals of any age or profession. It emphasizes the importance of recognizing the signs and intervening to support those who are suffering.

Strategies for Preventing and Addressing Cyberbullying:

Preventing cyberbullying requires a multi-faceted approach involving parents, educators, and society as a whole. Here are some strategies to consider:

Motivation and Inspiration:

In order to create a safer online environment, it is essential to develop effective strategies for preventing and addressing cyberbullying. This section provides actionable steps for individuals, parents, educators, and policymakers to tackle this issue head-on.

Real-Life Story: Emma's Empowerment

Emma, a high school student, decided to take a stand against cyberbullying after witnessing a classmate being targeted. She initiated a school-wide campaign to raise awareness about the issue, organizing workshops on responsible online behavior and the importance of digital empathy. Emma's efforts brought the school community together and empowered students to recognize their roles in preventing and addressing cyberbullying.

Emma's story highlights the power of proactive measures and the impact individuals can have in fostering a positive online culture.

Education and Awareness:

Raise awareness about cyberbullying through educational programs in schools, emphasizing the consequences of such behavior. Teach students about empathy, respect, and responsible digital citizenship.

Motivation:

As technology continues to evolve and shape our lives, it has become increasingly important to address the dark side of the digital world—cyberbullying and online harassment. In this chapter, we will explore the essential elements necessary to combat these issues effectively. Education and awareness are crucial tools that empower individuals to understand the consequences of their online actions, promote empathy, and foster a safe and inclusive digital environment.

Inspiration:

I was inspired to delve into this topic by a young woman named Sarah. Despite her vibrant personality and achievements, she suffered silently from relentless cyberbullying. The online abuse affected her self-esteem, mental health, and overall well-being. Witnessing Sarah's struggle, I became determined to shed light on cyberbullying and online harassment, offering practical solutions to eradicate this pervasive problem.

Real-Life Story:

In researching this chapter, I came across the story of Alex, a high school student. Alex was an avid gamer and enjoyed spending time online, immersing himself in various gaming communities. One day, he encountered a player who exhibited toxic behavior, insulting and mocking him relentlessly. At first, Alex brushed it off, considering it a one-time occurrence. However, the harassment escalated, with the player creating fake accounts to further torment Alex.

Feeling helpless and overwhelmed, Alex withdrew from his favorite online communities. The once-thriving gaming enthusiast became isolated and anxious, losing interest in activities he once enjoyed. Eventually, with the support of his parents and school counselor, he confronted the issue and reported the cyberbullying. The incident led to a thorough investigation, resulting in the identification and punishment of the perpetrator. This experience made Alex realize the importance of education and awareness in preventing cyberbullying and online harassment.

Open Communication:

Encourage open communication between teenagers and trusted adults, such as parents, teachers, or counselors. Create a safe space where victims can share their experiences without fear of judgment or reprisal.

Motivation:

Open communication plays a pivotal role in combating cyberbullying and online harassment. By fostering an environment where individuals feel comfortable discussing their experiences and concerns, we can break the cycle of silence and build a united front against online abuse.

Inspiration:

I drew inspiration for this section from my own experiences as a mentor to young adults. Through open conversations, I witnessed the transformative power of dialogue and the positive impact it had on building resilient and compassionate communities.

Real-Life Story:

During my mentoring sessions, I met a teenager named Mia who had fallen victim to cyberbullying. She hesitated to share her experience, fearing judgment and dismissal. However, with time and encouragement, Mia opened up about the emotional toll the harassment had taken on her. We discussed strategies to cope with cyberbullying and the importance of seeking support from trusted individuals. Through our ongoing conversations, Mia regained her confidence and found solace in knowing she was not alone.

Reporting and Intervention:

Establish clear reporting mechanisms for cyberbullying incidents. Encourage teenagers to report instances of online harassment to responsible authorities, such as school administrators or social media platforms, who can take appropriate action.

Motivation:

Reporting and intervention are critical components in combating cyberbullying and online harassment. It is essential to provide individuals with effective mechanisms to report abusive behavior and ensure appropriate action is taken promptly.

Inspiration:

My inspiration for this section stemmed from an encounter with an online community moderator named Mark. His dedication to creating a safe environment within the gaming community allowed him to intervene and address instances of cyberbullying effectively. Witnessing the positive impact Mark had on fostering a supportive digital space inspired me to explore reporting and intervention methods further.

Real-Life Story:

A young girl named Emily became a victim of relentless cyberbullying when her personal information was exposed online. Frightened and distraught, she reached out to the platform's support team, who took swift action by investigating the incident and promptly removing the content. Additionally, they provided Emily with resources to protect her online presence and offered emotional support throughout the process. This intervention not only helped Emily regain her sense of security but also instilled in her the confidence to advocate for a safer online environment.

Support Systems:

Develop support systems within schools and communities to provide counseling and resources for victims of cyberbullying. Offer guidance on coping strategies, building resilience, and fostering a sense of self-worth.

Motivation:

Support systems serve as pillars of strength for individuals affected by cyberbullying and online harassment. By establishing networks that provide emotional support, resources, and guidance, we can help victims navigate through challenging times and foster resilience.

Inspiration:

The resilience of survivors and the unwavering support they received from their loved ones served as a profound inspiration for this section. Witnessing the transformative power of compassionate support, I wanted to emphasize the importance of these networks in combating cyberbullying.

Real-Life Story:

Jacob, a college student, experienced cyberbullying throughout his academic journey. The persistent harassment took a toll on his mental health, and he contemplated dropping out of college. However, with the unwavering support of his friends, family, and university counselor, Jacob found the strength to persevere. They provided him with emotional support, guidance, and connected him with local support groups that specialized in cyberbullying prevention. This robust support system empowered Jacob to reclaim his sense of self-worth and pursue his dreams.

Promoting Digital Well-being and Responsible Online Behavior:

Promoting responsible online behavior can help prevent cyberbullying and create a positive digital environment. Consider the following approaches:

Motivation and Inspiration:

As the online world continues to evolve, it is vital to promote digital well-being and responsible online behavior. This section explores ways to create a healthier digital ecosystem, encouraging individuals to develop empathy, resilience, and ethical conduct online.

Real-Life Story: Alex's Transformation

Alex, a once avid participant in online harassment, experienced a life-altering realization when he saw the devastating consequences of his actions. Through therapy and introspection, he recognized the pain he had caused others and made a commitment to change. Alex started using his online platform to promote kindness and empathy, actively engaging in discussions about responsible online behavior.

Alex's story demonstrates the potential for personal growth and transformation, emphasizing the importance of empathy and ethical behavior in the digital realm.

Digital Literacy:

Educate teenagers about the potential risks and consequences of their online actions. Teach them about privacy settings, online etiquette, and the importance of critical thinking when consuming or sharing content.

In the age of technology, being digitally literate is essential for navigating the online world safely and responsibly. It involves understanding the potential risks and consequences of our actions online, as well as developing critical thinking skills to evaluate the credibility of information. Digital literacy empowers individuals to recognize and respond to cyberbullying effectively. By educating ourselves and others about online safety, privacy settings, and reporting mechanisms, we can become proactive agents in preventing and addressing cyberbullying incidents.

Real Life Story: Emma's Experience

Emma, a talented high school student, had always been passionate about art. She created a social media account to showcase her artwork and connect with fellow artists. Unfortunately, she quickly became the target of cyberbullying. People began leaving hurtful comments on her posts, criticizing her skills and appearance. Emma felt her confidence erode with every negative word.

However, Emma refused to be silenced. She embarked on a journey to enhance her digital literacy and learn about online safety measures. She discovered the importance of strong passwords, privacy settings, and the option to disable anonymous comments. Emma also familiarized herself with reporting tools on different platforms, empowering her to take action against cyberbullies. Through her newfound knowledge, she was able to create a safer space for herself and inspire others to do the same.

Empathy and Kindness:

Encourage teenagers to be empathetic and kind online. Teach them about the impact of their words and actions and the importance of treating others with respect, both online and offline.

In a world where screens shield us from face-to-face interactions, it is easy to forget that the people we encounter online are real individuals with feelings and emotions. Fostering empathy and kindness within ourselves and our online communities is crucial to combat cyberbullying. By treating others with respect, understanding, and compassion, we can create a culture of support and acceptance online.

Real Life Story: Jason's Journey

Jason was an avid gamer who spent a significant amount of time engaging with his online gaming community. One day, he witnessed a fellow player being relentlessly cyberbullied during a gaming session. Despite feeling torn between standing up against the bullies or remaining silent, Jason chose empathy and kindness. He intervened, defending the victim and urging others to join him. Gradually, the online community rallied around the victim, offering support and encouragement. Jason's actions inspired others to stand up against cyberbullying, creating a positive change within the gaming community.

Balance and Self-care:

Promote healthy digital habits by emphasizing the importance of balance and self-care. Encourage teenagers to take breaks from digital devices, engage in physical activities, and cultivate offline hobbies and friendships.

In the digital era, it is crucial to strike a balance between our online and offline lives. Spending excessive amounts of time online can make us more susceptible to cyberbullying, while neglecting our well-being. It is essential to disconnect periodically, engage in physical activities, and cultivate hobbies that foster our mental and emotional health. Taking care of ourselves empowers us to deal with cyberbullying more effectively and maintain a positive outlook.

Real Life Story: Sarah's Struggle

Sarah, a college student, found herself entangled in a web of cyberbullying that originated from her online social circle. The constant bombardment of hateful messages took a toll on her mental health, leading to anxiety and depression. However, Sarah sought solace and strength through self-care practices. She engaged in mindfulness exercises, sought support from her loved ones, and dedicated time to activities that brought her joy. Gradually, Sarah regained her self-confidence, emerged stronger, and became an advocate for promoting self-care in the face of cyberbullying.

Parental Involvement:

Parents should actively engage with their children's online activities, establish open lines of communication, and provide guidance on responsible online behavior. Encourage setting boundaries and monitoring online interactions without invading privacy.

Parents play a critical role in protecting their children from cyberbullying and teaching them responsible online behavior. By actively engaging in their children's digital lives, parents can monitor their online activities, educate them about potential risks, and foster open communication about any cyberbullying experiences. Providing guidance and support enables children to navigate the online world confidently and seek help when needed.

Real Life Story: John and His Son

John's son, Mark, became the victim of cyberbullying when he started middle school. As a concerned parent, John decided to learn about digital literacy and online safety to guide his son effectively. He established an open line of communication, encouraging Mark to share his experiences and concerns without fear of judgment. John also worked closely with the school to address the issue and promote anti-cyberbullying initiatives. Through their joint efforts, Mark not only overcame the cyberbullying he faced but also developed resilience and became an advocate for online safety within his school.

Conclusion:

Cyberbullying and online harassment pose significant challenges to teenagers' mental health and overall well-being. By understanding the nature and consequences of cyberbullying, recognizing the signs of online harassment, implementing prevention strategies, and promoting responsible digital behavior, we can work towards creating a safer and more supportive online environment. It requires a collaborative effort from parents, educators, policymakers, and teenagers themselves to build a digital landscape where kindness, empathy, and respect prevail.

Chapter 4

BODY IMAGE AND SELF-ESTEEM

Introduction:

In a society consumed by unrealistic beauty standards, teenagers often find themselves grappling with their body image and self-esteem. The relentless influence of media, advertising, and social media platforms can lead to a distorted perception of beauty and create immense pressure to conform. This chapter delves into the profound impact of societal beauty standards on teenagers, while emphasizing the importance of nurturing a positive body image and cultivating self-acceptance. By exploring strategies to build resilience in the face of media influences and promoting healthy habits and relationships with food and exercise, this chapter aims to empower teenagers to embrace their uniqueness and develop unshakeable self-esteem.

Motivation and Inspiration

In a world that places great emphasis on physical appearance, body image has become a significant concern for people of all ages. However, teenagers are particularly vulnerable to the influence of societal beauty standards, which can greatly impact their self-esteem and overall well-being. In this chapter, we will explore the complexities of body image, delve into the effects of societal beauty standards on teenagers, and discuss strategies for nurturing a positive body image, building self-esteem, and promoting healthy habits.

Real Life Story: Sarah's Journey to Self-Acceptance

Sarah was a bright and vivacious teenager with a contagious smile that could light up a room. However, beneath her cheerful facade, Sarah struggled with body image issues. Growing up in a society obsessed with unattainable beauty ideals, she often found herself comparing her appearance to the unrealistic standards portrayed in the media. She felt pressure to conform to a certain body type and was constantly plagued by negative thoughts about her own body.

The turning point in Sarah's life came during her sophomore year of high school. One day, while scrolling through social media, she stumbled upon an article that shed light on the damaging effects of societal beauty standards. Sarah discovered that many of the images she had internalized as the epitome of beauty were heavily photoshopped, creating an unattainable ideal. This revelation sparked her curiosity to dig deeper into the topic and find ways to break free from the shackles of negative body image.

Section 1: Societal Beauty Standards and Their Impact on Teenagers

In today's society, teenagers are bombarded with images and messages that portray unrealistic beauty standards. Media platforms, advertisements, and social media often emphasize narrow definitions of attractiveness, leading many teenagers to feel pressure to conform to these ideals. The constant exposure to these images can have detrimental effects on their body image and self-esteem.

1.1 The Influence of Media and Advertising

The portrayal of idealized bodies in media and advertising

The use of photo editing and airbrushing techniques

The impact of comparing oneself to digitally altered images

The perpetuation of unattainable beauty standards

1.2 The Role of Social Media

The curated nature of social media and its impact on self-perception

The influence of likes, comments, and followers on self-worth

The prevalence of appearance-focused content and filters

The potential for cyberbullying and negative comparisons

Motivation and Inspiration:

As teenagers navigate the complex world of adolescence, they often find themselves confronted with unrealistic societal beauty standards. The pressure to conform to these standards can take a toll on their self-esteem and body image. In this chapter, we will delve into the impact of societal beauty standards on teenagers and explore ways to nurture a positive body image and self-acceptance. By promoting healthy habits and relationships with food and exercise, we aim to empower teenagers to build resilience in the face of media influences and develop a strong sense of self-esteem.

Real Life Story: Embracing Individuality

Samantha was a vibrant and creative 16-year-old girl. She possessed a natural talent for painting and had a knack for making people laugh with her witty remarks. However, as she entered her teenage years, Samantha began to feel a constant pressure to conform to society's narrow definition of beauty. The glossy magazines she leafed through and the seemingly perfect images she saw on social media left her feeling inadequate and self-conscious.

Samantha's turning point came when she stumbled upon an interview with a famous artist who defied conventional beauty norms. The artist spoke passionately about the importance of embracing one's individuality and celebrating unique features. Inspired by this message, Samantha made a conscious decision to focus on her artistic abilities rather than her physical appearance.

Section 2: Nurturing a Positive Body Image and Self-acceptance

To counteract the negative effects of societal beauty standards, it is crucial to promote a positive body image and foster self-acceptance among teenagers.

By cultivating a healthy relationship with their bodies, teenagers can develop a strong sense of self and improve their overall well-being.

2.1 Embracing Body Diversity and Individuality

Encouraging acceptance of different body shapes, sizes, and appearances

Highlighting the beauty of diversity and uniqueness

Challenging stereotypes and promoting inclusivity

2.2 Developing Self-Compassion and Acceptance

Practicing self-compassion and positive self-talk

Fostering self-acceptance and embracing imperfections

Recognizing and challenging negative thoughts and self-judgment

Cultivating gratitude for the body's capabilities and functions

Societal beauty standards can be suffocating, making teenagers feel like they need to achieve an unattainable ideal. It's essential to guide them towards embracing their uniqueness and cultivating a positive body image. Encourage open and honest conversations about beauty, emphasizing that it comes in various shapes, sizes, and forms.

Parents, mentors, and educators play a crucial role in creating a safe space for teenagers to explore their identities without judgment. By fostering an environment that celebrates diversity and promotes self-acceptance, we can empower teenagers to develop a positive body image.

Section 3: Building Self-esteem and Resilience in the Face of Media Influences

To combat the negative impact of media influences, it is essential to empower teenagers to develop a strong sense of self-esteem and resilience. By building a foundation of self-worth that goes beyond external appearance, teenagers can withstand societal pressures and develop a positive self-image.

3.1 Recognizing Inner Qualities and Strengths

Shifting the focus from external appearance to internal qualities and talents

Encouraging self-discovery and nurturing individual strengths

Promoting a sense of accomplishment and pride in personal achievements

3.2 Cultivating Positive Support Systems

Building healthy relationships and connections that value individuals for who they are

Surrounding oneself with positive influences and supportive friends

Seeking guidance from trusted adults and mentors

Section 4: Promoting Healthy Habits and Relationships with Food and Exercise

In addition to body image, a positive relationship with food and exercise is crucial for overall well-being. By promoting healthy habits and a balanced approach, teenagers can maintain physical health while fostering a positive body image.

4.1 Education on Nutrition and Body Needs

Providing accurate information about nutrition and the body's needs

Encouraging balanced and mindful eating habits

Discouraging restrictive diets and promoting intuitive eating

4.2 Promoting Enjoyable Physical Activities

Encouraging physical activities that focus on enjoyment rather than appearance

Highlighting the mental and emotional benefits of exercise

Discouraging exercise as a means of punishment or weight control

Media influences can profoundly impact a teenager's self-esteem. Airbrushed photos, filters, and digitally enhanced images distort reality, making it essential to teach teenagers how to critically analyze and challenge these unrealistic representations.

Encourage teenagers to focus on their strengths and talents rather than fixating on their perceived flaws. Engage them in activities that boost their confidence and provide a sense of achievement. By helping teenagers build resilience and a strong sense of self, they can overcome the negativity and comparison trap perpetuated by societal beauty standards.

Promoting Healthy Habits and Relationships:

Promoting healthy habits and relationships with food and exercise is vital for teenagers' overall well-being. Encourage a balanced approach to nutrition, emphasizing the importance of nourishing their bodies rather than adhering to restrictive diets. Encourage physical activities that teenagers genuinely enjoy and help them discover the joy of movement beyond appearance-based goals.

Foster open discussions about body positivity, mental health, and the impact of media on self-image. Teach teenagers to question and challenge beauty standards that prioritize outward appearance over inner qualities and character.

Conclusion:

Developing a positive body image and self-esteem is a journey that requires ongoing support and effort. By understanding the impact of societal beauty standards, nurturing self-acceptance, building resilience, and promoting healthy habits, teenagers can develop a strong sense of self-worth and navigate the pressures of modern society with confidence and grace. It

Chapter 5

SUBSTANCE ABUSE: UNDERSTANDING, PREVENTION, AND RECOVERY

Introduction:

Substance abuse among teenagers is a complex issue that can have severe consequences on their physical health, mental well-being, and overall development. In this chapter, we will delve into the motivations behind substance abuse, how to recognize signs of addiction, strategies for prevention, and the importance of seeking professional help and resources for recovery.

Motivation, Inspiration, and Real Life Story

In this chapter, we delve into the complex world of substance abuse, a pervasive issue that affects countless individuals, families, and communities. Our motivation to explore this topic stems from a deep desire to understand the underlying causes behind substance abuse among teenagers and provide insights into prevention strategies, recognizing signs of addiction, and seeking professional help and resources for recovery. We draw inspiration from the countless individuals who have bravely fought their battles with substance abuse and emerged on the other side, offering hope and inspiration to those still trapped in its grip.

Real Life Story: Sarah's Journey

Sarah was a bright and ambitious teenager with dreams of becoming a successful artist. She had a loving family, supportive friends, and seemingly everything going for her. However, as she entered high school, she faced mounting pressures and stressors that gradually began to take a toll on her mental health. Fearing failure and struggling to cope with academic expectations, Sarah found solace in alcohol and drugs.

What began as an occasional escape soon turned into a full-fledged addiction. Sarah's motivation to use substances was driven by a desperate need to numb her pain and find temporary relief from her overwhelming emotions. The substances seemed to provide a temporary escape from the pressures she faced, creating a false sense of comfort and security.

Recognizing the Signs

Sarah's story is just one example of how substance abuse can take hold of a young person's life. It is crucial to recognize the signs and symptoms of substance abuse early on to intervene and offer support. Some common signs include changes in behavior, sudden mood swings, declining academic performance, isolation from friends and family, secretive behavior, and physical changes such as bloodshot eyes or unexplained weight loss.

Prevention Strategies and Supportive Environments

Preventing substance abuse among teenagers requires a multifaceted approach that involves creating supportive environments and implementing effective strategies. Education plays a vital role in prevention, as it equips young people with the knowledge and skills to make informed decisions. Schools, parents, and communities must come together to promote healthy coping mechanisms, foster open dialogue, and provide positive role models.

Additionally, creating supportive environments that prioritize mental health and well-being can greatly reduce the risk of substance abuse. By addressing the underlying causes of stress and offering accessible resources, we can empower teenagers to navigate life's challenges without resorting to substances.

Seeking Professional Help and Resources for Recovery

Recognizing that substance abuse is a complex issue that often requires professional intervention is crucial. Sarah's journey towards recovery only began when she acknowledged her addiction and sought help. Professional resources such as therapists, counselors, and support groups can provide the necessary tools and guidance for individuals struggling with substance abuse.

It is essential to understand that recovery is a lifelong process. Building a strong support system, including family, friends, and mentors, is vital for sustained recovery. By sharing Sarah's story and exploring the motivations behind substance abuse, we hope to inspire others to seek help, break the cycle of addiction, and reclaim their lives.

Section 1: Understanding the Motivations behind Substance Abuse

1.1 Social and Peer Influences:

The role of peer pressure and the desire to fit in.

Influence of social norms and perceptions about substance use.

Coping mechanisms for stress, anxiety, and emotional difficulties.

1.2 Self-Medication and Emotional Escape:

Substance abuse as a way to cope with underlying mental health issues.

Seeking temporary relief or escape from problems or painful experiences.

The cycle of substance use and self-destructive behaviors.

1.3 Curiosity and Experimentation:

Natural curiosity and the desire to explore new experiences.

Lack of awareness about the potential risks and consequences of substance abuse.

The importance of education and raising awareness about the dangers of substance use.

Behind Substance Abuse Among Teenagers

Motivation is the driving force behind any behavior, including substance abuse. To effectively address the issue, we must delve into the underlying factors that lead teenagers down this path. The desire to fit in, peer pressure, curiosity, and self-medication for emotional or psychological pain are among the common motivations.

Real-Life Story: Emily's Struggle

Emily, a bright and talented teenager, grew up in a broken home. Her parents' divorce left her feeling lost and abandoned. Seeking solace, she started hanging out with a group of friends who frequently indulged in drugs and alcohol. In this environment, substance abuse became a means to numb the pain and escape from her troubles. Understanding Emily's motivations helps us empathize with her struggle and recognize that substance abuse often stems from deeper issues.

Section 2: Recognizing Signs of Substance Abuse and Addiction

2.1 Behavioral and Physical Signs:

Changes in behavior, such as sudden mood swings, irritability, or aggression.

Decline in academic performance, increased absenteeism, or lack of interest.

Physical signs like bloodshot eyes, changes in appetite or sleep patterns.

2.2 Emotional and Psychological Signs:

Increased secrecy, isolation, or withdrawal from friends and family.

Unexplained financial difficulties or stealing to support substance abuse.

Emotional instability, depression, anxiety, or heightened paranoia.

2.3 Identifying Addiction:

Understanding the distinction between substance abuse and addiction.

Dependence and tolerance as indicators of addiction.

The progressive nature of addiction and its impact on physical and mental health.

Recognizing the signs of substance abuse is crucial for early intervention and support. Adolescence is a time of rapid physical, emotional, and social changes, making it difficult to differentiate between normal behavior and addiction. Key signs include sudden changes in behavior, academic decline, withdrawal from family and friends, secretive behavior, and physical symptoms like bloodshot eyes and changes in appetite.

Real-Life Story: Alex's Battle

Alex was an outgoing and popular teenager who excelled in academics and sports. However, his friends began noticing a shift in his behavior. He became increasingly isolated, his grades plummeted, and he started neglecting his appearance. Alex's friends, recognizing these signs as potential substance abuse, confronted him and encouraged him to seek help. Their intervention proved crucial in saving him from a downward spiral.

Section 3: Prevention Strategies and Creating Supportive Environments

3.1 Building Resilience and Life Skills:

Promoting healthy coping mechanisms and stress management techniques.

Developing strong interpersonal skills and decision-making abilities.

Providing education on the risks and consequences of substance abuse.

3.2 Strengthening Support Systems:

Fostering open communication and trust between teenagers and adults.

Encouraging positive peer influences and supportive friendships.

Involvement of parents, schools, and communities in prevention efforts.

3.3 Creating Safe and Drug-Free Environments:

Implementing and enforcing policies and regulations related to substance use.

Organizing drug awareness campaigns and prevention programs in schools.

Encouraging extracurricular activities and hobbies that promote healthy lifestyles.

Preventing substance abuse requires a multi-faceted approach that involves creating supportive environments and empowering teenagers with the knowledge and skills to make healthy choices. Building strong connections with family, friends, and positive role models can act as protective factors. Educating teenagers about the risks and consequences of substance abuse, teaching them coping mechanisms, and fostering open communication channels are essential components of prevention strategies.

Real-Life Story: The Power of a Supportive Community

Sarah, a teenager struggling with low self-esteem and loneliness, found solace in a community center that offered after-school programs and mentorship. Through positive role models and engaging activities, Sarah gained a sense of belonging and purpose. The supportive environment provided her with the tools to resist substance abuse and make positive life choices.

Section 4: Seeking Professional Help and Resources for Recovery

4.1 Recognizing the Need for Help:

Overcoming the barriers to seeking help, including stigma and denial.

Encouraging open conversations about substance abuse and mental health.

Normalizing the seeking of professional assistance for addiction.

4.2 Treatment Options:

Overview of different treatment approaches, including therapy and counseling.

Exploring rehabilitation programs, detoxification, and residential treatment.

Incorporating support groups, such as 12-step programs or group therapy.

4.3 Support and Aftercare:

Recovery from substance abuse often requires professional intervention and access to resources. Encouraging teenagers to seek help, whether through school counselors, therapists, or addiction helplines, is crucial. Equally important is the role of family and friends in providing unwavering support and understanding during the recovery journey. Rehabilitation centers, support groups, and community organizations also play a vital role in helping teenagers regain control of their lives.

Real-Life Story: Mark's Transformation

Mark battled with addiction for several years, causing severe strain on his relationships and overall well-being. Finally, he sought professional help and entered a rehabilitation program. With the support of his family, therapy, and participation in support groups, Mark was able to rebuild his life and pursue his passions. Today, he shares his story to inspire others and provide hope for those facing similar challenges.

Conclusion:

Substance abuse among teenagers is a complex issue influenced by various factors. Understanding the motivations behind substance abuse, recognizing signs of addiction, implementing prevention strategies, and seeking professional help and resources for recovery are vital steps in addressing this issue. By creating supportive environments and fostering open dialogue, we can provide teenagers with the necessary tools and support to overcome substance abuse and lead healthy, fulfilling lives.

Chapter 6

RELATIONSHIP ISSUES AND DATING VIOLENCE

Introduction:

Navigating relationships is a fundamental aspect of adolescent development. However, it is crucial for teenagers to understand what constitutes a healthy relationship and how to recognize signs of potential harm. This chapter delves deep into relationship issues and dating violence, focusing on the importance of healthy communication, consent, and boundaries. We will explore different forms of dating violence and abuse, and provide resources and support for both victims and bystanders.

Motivation and Inspiration

Relationships are an integral part of our lives. They bring joy, companionship, and support, but they can also present challenges and obstacles. In this chapter, we delve into the crucial topic of relationship issues and dating violence. Our motivation stems from a deep desire to promote healthy and respectful relationships, as well as provide support to those who may be experiencing or witnessing dating violence.

Inspiration for this chapter comes from the countless individuals who have shared their stories and experiences, shedding light on the prevalence and devastating consequences of dating violence. Their courage and resilience drive us to educate and empower others, ensuring that nobody has to suffer in silence or endure abuse within their relationships.

Real-Life Story: Emily's Journey

Emily was a bright and ambitious college student, known for her radiant smile and caring nature. She was excited to explore new horizons, both academically and personally. Like many young adults, she sought companionship and began dating Mark, a charming and seemingly caring individual.

At first, their relationship blossomed, and Emily felt like she had found her soulmate. However, as time passed, subtle signs of control and manipulation emerged. Mark would frequently criticize Emily's appearance, belittle her achievements, and isolate her from her friends and family. The once vibrant and confident Emily began to doubt herself and question her worth.

It wasn't until Emily attended a workshop on healthy relationships that she realized the red flags within her own partnership. She discovered the importance of consent, communication, and establishing boundaries.

Emily mustered the courage to confide in a close friend, who provided unwavering support and connected her to resources for victims of dating violence.

Section 1: Navigating Healthy Relationships

1.1 Understanding Healthy Relationships:

The characteristics of healthy relationships based on respect, trust, and equality.

The importance of open communication, mutual support, and compromise.

Recognizing the value of individuality and personal growth within a relationship.

1.2 Recognizing Red Flags:

Identifying warning signs of potentially unhealthy or abusive relationships.

Red flags related to control, jealousy, possessiveness, and isolation.

The role of gut instincts and intuition in recognizing problematic dynamics.

Understanding what constitutes a healthy relationship is vital to avoiding the pitfalls of dating violence. Healthy relationships are built on mutual respect, trust, and open communication. They empower individuals to express themselves and pursue their goals while supporting their partner's aspirations. However, it's essential to be aware of the red flags that indicate a relationship may be heading towards an unhealthy or abusive path.

Some common red flags include controlling behavior, possessiveness, jealousy, verbal insults, belittling, isolation from friends and family, threats, physical aggression, and pressure to engage in activities against one's will. By recognizing these warning signs, individuals can take proactive steps to protect themselves and seek help if necessary.

Section 2: Promoting Consent, Communication, and Boundaries

2.1 The Concept of Consent:

Defining consent and the importance of enthusiastic, ongoing consent.

Discussing consent within various contexts, including physical intimacy and digital interactions.

Understanding the impact of power imbalances on consent.

2.2 Effective Communication:

Emphasizing the significance of open and honest communication in relationships.

Developing active listening skills and fostering empathy.

Encouraging assertiveness and respectful conflict resolution.

2.3 Establishing Boundaries:

Understanding personal boundaries and their role in maintaining healthy relationships.

Discussing different types of boundaries: physical, emotional, and digital.

Asserting boundaries and responding to boundary violations.

Promoting Consent, Communication, and Boundaries

Consent, communication, and boundaries are essential pillars of healthy relationships. Consent means that both partners freely and willingly agree to engage in any sexual activity or romantic gesture. Clear and ongoing communication allows partners to express their needs, desires, and concerns openly. Establishing and respecting personal boundaries ensures that individuals feel safe, both emotionally and physically, within the relationship.

Section 3: Understanding Different Forms of Dating Violence and Abuse

3.1 Physical Abuse:

Defining physical abuse and recognizing signs of physical violence in relationships.

The cycle of violence and the importance of immediate safety measures.

Highlighting the significance of legal consequences and reporting incidents.

3.2 Emotional and Psychological Abuse:

Identifying emotional and psychological abuse, including manipulation and control tactics.

The long-lasting effects of emotional abuse on self-esteem and mental health.

Encouraging individuals to seek support and validation for their experiences.

3.3 Digital Abuse:

Examining the impact of technology on dating violence, such as cyberstalking or harassment.

Recognizing digital red flags, including non-consensual sharing of explicit content.

Promoting online safety and responsible digital citizenship.

Dating violence and abuse can take various forms, including physical, emotional, verbal, sexual, and digital abuse. Physical abuse involves any form of physical harm or threats, such as hitting, pushing, or restraining someone. Emotional abuse includes manipulation, constant criticism, gaslighting, and demeaning behavior. Verbal abuse involves using words to control, belittle, or intimidate a partner. Sexual abuse encompasses any non-consensual sexual activity or pressure. Digital abuse refers to the use of technology to control or harass a partner, such as monitoring their online activities or spreading explicit images without consent.

Section 4: Providing Resources and Support for Victims and Bystanders

4.1 Seeking Help:

Encouraging victims to reach out to trusted adults, friends, or helpline services.

Discussing the importance of confidentiality and non-judgmental support.

Highlighting available resources such as counseling, support groups, and hotlines.

4.2 Intervening as Bystanders:

Educating bystanders on their role in preventing and addressing dating violence.

Strategies for intervening safely and supporting victims without putting oneself at risk.

Promoting a culture of empathy, respect, and bystander intervention.

4.3 Promoting Prevention and Education:

The significance of comprehensive sex education that includes discussions on healthy relationships and consent.

Engaging schools and communities in prevention programs and awareness campaigns.

Advocating for policy changes and funding for organizations addressing dating violence.

For victims of dating violence, it is essential to know that help is available. Organizations, hotlines, and support groups offer resources and assistance to those who have experienced abuse. It is crucial for victims to reach out to trusted friends, family members, or professionals who can provide support and guidance.

Bystanders also play a crucial role in ending dating violence. By recognizing signs of abuse and offering support to those affected, they can help break the cycle of violence. Bystanders can intervene safely, offer a listening ear, encourage victims to seek help, and educate others about healthy relationships.

Motivation and Inspiration:

In a world where relationships play a vital role in our lives, it is essential to navigate healthy connections and understand the signs of trouble. Dating violence and abusive relationships can have a devastating impact on individuals, and it is crucial to shed light on these issues. This chapter aims to empower readers by providing knowledge about healthy relationships, red flags, consent, communication, boundaries, and various forms of dating violence. By doing so, we can create awareness, encourage positive change, and promote a culture of respect and support.

Real Life Story: Emily's Journey

Emily was an ambitious and bright young woman in her early twenties. She had dreams of pursuing a successful career and finding love. Like many others, Emily believed that relationships were built on trust, mutual respect, and love. Unfortunately, her journey towards a healthy relationship was not without obstacles.

During her second year of college, Emily met Mark, a charming and charismatic guy. They quickly formed a connection, and Emily fell head over heels in love. Initially, everything seemed perfect. Mark was attentive, showering Emily with affection and compliments. But as time went on, subtle signs of trouble began to emerge.

Mark gradually became possessive, wanting to know Emily's every move and controlling her interactions with friends and family. He would manipulate her emotions, making her feel guilty for spending time with anyone other than him. These signs of emotional abuse slowly eroded Emily's self-esteem, leaving her feeling trapped and isolated.

Emily's friends and family noticed the changes in her behavior, but she was too deep in the relationship to recognize the warning signs herself. It was during a casual conversation with her best friend, Sarah, that Emily began to realize the severity of her situation. Sarah shared stories of healthy relationships, emphasizing the importance of open communication, trust, and respect.

Inspired by her friend's words, Emily decided to seek guidance and support. She reached out to a counselor at her college, who introduced her to a support group for victims of dating violence. This group provided a safe space for Emily to share her experiences, learn from others, and gain the strength to break free from the toxic relationship.

With the help of the support group and professional counseling, Emily started her journey of healing and self-discovery. She learned about the different forms of dating violence, including emotional, physical, and sexual abuse. Recognizing the red flags in her past relationship, Emily gained the tools to establish healthy boundaries and communicate her needs effectively.

Through her own experience and newfound knowledge, Emily became an advocate for healthy relationships and dating violence awareness. She dedicated her time to educating others about the signs of abuse and providing resources for victims and bystanders. Emily's journey not only transformed her life but also inspired others to seek help and break the cycle of violence.

Navigating Healthy Relationships and Recognizing Red Flags:

Emily's story highlights the importance of understanding what constitutes a healthy relationship. It is crucial to recognize red flags early on, such as possessiveness, isolation from loved ones, manipulation, and lack of respect for boundaries. By being aware of these warning signs, individuals can protect themselves from entering or continuing toxic relationships.

Promoting Consent, Communication, and Boundaries:

Consent, communication, and boundaries are the cornerstones of healthy relationships. Understanding and respecting each other's boundaries fosters a sense of trust and emotional safety. Effective communication allows partners to express their needs, desires, and concerns openly. Promoting consent ensures that all interactions are consensual and mutually agreed upon, establishing a foundation of respect and equality.

Understanding Different Forms of Dating Violence and Abuse:

Dating violence encompasses various forms of abuse, including emotional, physical, sexual, and digital abuse. It is essential to be aware of these forms and understand their impact on victims. By increasing awareness, we can provide support and resources for individuals experiencing such abuse and work towards preventing it in our communities.

Providing Resources and Support for Victims and Bystanders:

Empathy, support, and resources are vital for victims of dating violence. Organizations and helplines dedicated to helping victims are available in many communities. By providing these resources, we can empower victims to seek help and support their journey towards healing. Additionally, bystanders play a crucial role in supporting victims and preventing future abuse by speaking up, offering assistance, and encouraging conversations about healthy relationships.

Conclusion:

By understanding the dynamics of healthy relationships, promoting consent and communication, recognizing different forms of dating violence, and providing support for victims and bystanders, we can work towards creating safer and more respectful environments for teenagers. It is essential to empower teenagers with knowledge, resources, and support systems, enabling them to build and maintain healthy relationships while recognizing and addressing harmful behaviors. Through education, awareness, and collective efforts, we can strive for a future where dating violence becomes a thing of the past. Emily's journey and the lessons learned from her experiences serve as an inspiration for all of us. Navigating healthy relationships, recognizing red flags, promoting consent and communication, understanding different forms of dating violence, and providing resources and support are crucial steps in creating a safer and more respectful society. By educating ourselves and others about these issues, we can make a difference and foster a culture of love, respect, and support in our relationships.

Chapter 7

——◦◦◦——

CREATING A SUPPORTIVE ENVIRONMENT

Introduction:

Creating a supportive environment is essential for promoting the mental health and well-being of teenagers. In this chapter, we will delve deeper into the roles of parents, educators, and communities in supporting teenage mental health. We will explore the importance of fostering open communication and safe spaces for discussion, promoting mental health literacy and awareness, and implementing school-based programs and initiatives. By understanding the underlying thoughts and reasons behind the challenges teenagers face, we can work towards effective solutions.

Motivation and Inspiration

In a world where the mental health of teenagers is increasingly at risk, it is imperative to create a supportive environment that nurtures their well-being. Adolescence is a vulnerable and transformative period, marked by various challenges and pressures. Parents, educators, and communities have a vital role to play in fostering the mental health of teenagers. By providing a safe and supportive space, promoting open communication, and raising awareness about mental health, we can empower the younger generation to thrive and overcome the obstacles they face.

Real-Life Story: Sarah's Journey

Sarah was a bright and ambitious teenager who seemed to have it all. She excelled academically, participated in extracurricular activities, and had a close-knit group of friends. However, beneath her seemingly perfect exterior, Sarah was silently struggling with her mental health. The pressure to excel and meet societal expectations took a toll on her well-being.

Fortunately, Sarah's parents noticed a change in her behavior and decided to intervene. They created an environment where open communication was encouraged, providing Sarah with a safe space to express her feelings. They listened without judgment and sought professional help when needed. This support system played a crucial role in Sarah's journey towards recovery.

The Role of Parents:

Parents play a crucial role in supporting their teenagers' mental health. It is important for parents to cultivate a supportive and non-judgmental environment at home. Some key approaches parents can take *include:*

Active listening: Listening attentively to their teenagers' concerns, thoughts, and emotions without judgment or interruption.

Validation: Validating their teenagers' experiences and feelings, acknowledging their struggles, and offering empathy and understanding.

Providing resources: Ensuring teenagers have access to mental health resources, such as therapy, support groups, or helplines.

Modeling healthy behaviors: Demonstrating healthy coping mechanisms, stress management, and self-care practices.

Parents, educators, and communities have a pivotal role in supporting teenage mental health. Their collective efforts can create a supportive environment that fosters emotional well-being and resilience. Here are some key aspects of their role:

Fostering Open Communication and Safe Spaces for Discussion

Parents, educators, and communities need to create safe spaces for teenagers to express their thoughts and feelings without fear of judgment or retribution. Open and non-judgmental communication channels can facilitate early identification of mental health concerns and provide a platform for seeking help. This could involve regular check-ins, family meetings, or school-based support groups where teenagers can share their experiences and concerns.

Promoting Mental Health Literacy and Awareness

Parents, educators, and communities must prioritize mental health literacy and awareness. This involves providing accurate information about mental health, debunking myths, and educating themselves and others about common mental health challenges faced by teenagers. By understanding the signs and symptoms of mental health issues, they can offer appropriate support and connect teenagers with professional help when needed.

The Role of Educators:

Educators have a unique opportunity to create a supportive environment within schools. They can contribute to teenagers' mental health and well-being through the following approaches:

Mental health education: Incorporating mental health literacy into the curriculum, teaching students about coping strategies, stress management, and emotional well-being.

Safe spaces: Creating safe and inclusive spaces within the school where students can express their thoughts, concerns, and emotions without fear of judgment.

Building connections: Fostering positive relationships with students and being approachable and supportive when they need guidance or assistance.

Implementing School-Based Programs and Initiatives

Educators and school administrators play a vital role in creating a supportive environment within educational institutions. Schools can implement mental health programs and initiatives that address the unique needs of teenagers. This could include workshops on stress management, resilience-building exercises, and teaching coping skills. Furthermore, school counselors can be trained to recognize and respond to mental health concerns effectively.

Collaboration: Collaborating with mental health professionals, parents, and the community to implement effective strategies and programs.

Fostering Open Communication and Safe Spaces for

Discussion: Open communication is vital for teenagers to feel comfortable seeking support. Here are some ways to promote open communication and

Create safe spaces: Encouraging dialogue: Encourage open and honest conversations about mental health, emotions, and challenges without judgment or stigma.

Active listening: Actively listen to teenagers, validate their experiences, and offer support and guidance when needed.

Peer support: Facilitate peer support groups or mentoring programs where teenagers can connect with others who may be going through similar experiences.

Anonymous reporting systems: Implement anonymous reporting systems to report bullying, harassment, or concerns about mental health without fear of retaliation.

Promoting Mental Health Literacy and Awareness:

Promoting mental health literacy among teenagers is crucial for early intervention and support. Some strategies to promote mental health literacy include:

Education campaigns: Organize awareness campaigns, workshops, and presentations to educate teenagers about common mental health issues, warning signs, and available resources.

Media literacy: Teach teenagers to critically analyze media portrayals of mental health and help them understand the difference between reality and idealized representations.

Destigmatization: Challenge stigmas surrounding mental health by openly discussing it, sharing personal stories of resilience, and promoting empathy and understanding.

Implementing School-Based Programs and Initiatives:

Schools can play a significant role in implementing programs and initiatives to support teenagers' mental health. Some effective approaches include:

Mental health screening: Conduct regular mental health screenings to identify students who may need additional support.

Peer support programs: Establish peer support programs where older students or trained peer mentors can provide guidance and support to their peers.

Counseling services: Ensure access to qualified mental health professionals within the school setting, offering individual or group counseling sessions.

Stress management programs: Implement stress reduction programs that include relaxation techniques, mindfulness exercises, and time management skills.

Collaboration with Community Resources

Communities need to come together to support teenagers' mental health. This can involve partnering with mental health organizations, local clinics, and support groups to provide resources and services. By establishing connections with these resources, parents, educators, and communities can ensure that teenagers have access to the help they need when facing mental health challenges.

Conclusion:

Creating a supportive environment for teenagers requires a collaborative effort from parents, educators, and communities. By fostering open communication, promoting mental health literacy, and implementing school-based programs and initiatives, we can provide the necessary support and resources for teenagers to navigate their mental health challenges successfully. By addressing the underlying thoughts and reasons behind these challenges, we can work towards long-lasting solutions that promote the well-being and resilience of teenagers in today's society.

Dear Readers,

I am writing this message with immense gratitude and a sense of deep appreciation for your support and engagement with my book on the critical topic of mental health issues faced by teenagers. It is an honor to have the opportunity to shed light on these often overlooked challenges that our young generation confronts.

In today's fast-paced world, teenagers are increasingly burdened by mental health problems such as anxiety, depression, and stress. Academic pressure, the influence of social media, bullying, and the overall demands of modern life contribute to their struggles. By delving into these issues, we hope to raise awareness and encourage open conversations that will lead to positive change.

One crucial area we explored in the book is cyberbullying and online harassment, which have become distressingly common among teenagers. The emotional and psychological impact of such behaviors cannot be underestimated. By addressing and preventing cyberbullying through the combined efforts of parents, schools, and society, we can create a safer and more compassionate digital environment.

Another pressing concern we addressed is the issue of body image and self-esteem. Teenagers face immense pressure to conform to unrealistic beauty standards perpetuated by the media and social platforms. This pressure often leads to body image issues and low self-esteem. By promoting body positivity, self-acceptance, and media literacy, we aim to empower teenagers to embrace their individuality and cultivate healthy self-perceptions.

Substance abuse remains a persistent challenge for teenagers, driven by factors such as peer pressure, curiosity, and attempts to cope with stress or emotional difficulties. In our book, we emphasize the importance of education, early intervention, and creating supportive environments to prevent substance abuse and provide the necessary assistance to those struggling with addiction.

Additionally, we delve into relationship issues and dating violence, offering insights into consent, healthy communication, and recognizing signs of abuse. By equipping teenagers with the knowledge and resources to navigate romantic relationships safely, we strive to promote healthy relationship dynamics and provide support for those facing dating violence.

To address these issues effectively, we emphasize the significance of open communication, education, and fostering supportive environments. It is our collective responsibility as a society to create safe spaces for discussion and provide the necessary support systems that cater to the unique needs of teenagers.

Once again, I extend my heartfelt appreciation to each and every one of you for joining me on this journey and engaging with these critical topics. Together, we can work towards a future where teenagers feel understood, supported, and empowered to overcome the challenges they face. Your commitment to spreading awareness and fostering positive change is truly inspiring.

With sincere gratitude,

Piyush Raj

"Ready to get personalized advice for your unique needs? Contact our team of experts today and schedule a free consultation. Let us help you find the solutions you've been searching for!"

SCAN THIS OR CODE AND BOOK FOR FREE!!